PUSHKIN PRESS

'Easily digestible . . . a book that ultimately lives longer in the memory than the hour or so it takes to read'

Financial Times

'A lovely coming-of-age story about a boy who becomes obsessed with a woman who sells sandwiches'

Bustle

'In Louise Heal Kawai's translation the novella is a wonderful example of the power of narrative voice'

Japan Times

'Whimsical ... Described as Haruki Murakami's "favorite young novelist", Kawakami is destined to charm Anglophone audiences as well'

Library Journal

'Mieko Kawakami is a master of the novella ... A moving and surprisingly funny tale of growing up and learning how to lose, it is no overstatement to assert that *Ms Ice Sandwich* is Mieko Kawakami at her very best ... Very highly recommended'

Midwest Book Review

'The narrator's perspective is so singular and well-crafted that *Ms Ice Sandwich*'s message about the ephemerality of human connection is never in any danger of becoming trite and sentimental'

Contemporary Japanese Literature

'A warm, heart-melting story ... a treat'

The Straits Times

'A touching novella ... *Ms Ice Sandwich* interrogates what it means to love and lose'

Culture Trip

'Delightful . . . Kawakami's dialogue, fluidly rendered into English by Louise Heal Kawai, captures beautifully and with great humor the eager dynamism of a child's mind'

World Literature Today

Born in Osaka prefecture in 1976, **MIEKO KAWAKAMI** began her career as a singer and songwriter before making her literary debut in 2006. Her first novella *My Ego, My Teeth, and the World*, published in 2007, was nominated for the Akutagawa Prize and awarded the Tsubouchi Shoyo Prize for Young Emerging Writers. The following year, Kawakami published *Breasts and Eggs* as a short novella. It won the Akutagawa Prize, Japan's most prestigious literary honour, and earned praise from the acclaimed writer Yoko Ogawa. Kawakami's work has been widely translated, and she is the author of the novels *Heaven*, *The Night Belongs to Lovers*, and the newly expanded *Breasts and Eggs*, her first novel to be published in English. She lives in Japan.

LOUISE HEAL KAWAI has translated around a dozen works of Japanese literature, including works by Seicho Matsumoto and Taeko Tomioka. In 2018, her translation of *Seventeen* by Hideo Yokoyama was longlisted for the Best Translated Book Award. Her most recent works for Pushkin are the classic locked-room murder mysteries *Murder in the Crooked House* by Soji Shimada and Seishi Yokomizo's *The Honjin Murders*. Louise lives in Japan's Kanto region.

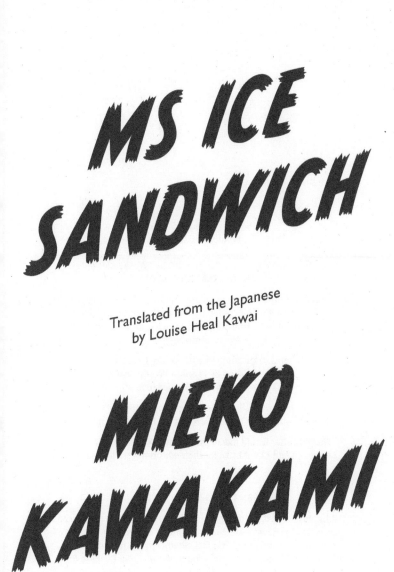

MS ICE SANDWICH

Translated from the Japanese
by Louise Heal Kawai

MIEKO KAWAKAMI

PUSHKIN PRESS

Pushkin Press
Somerset House, Strand
London WC2R 1LA

Original title: "Misu Aisu Sandoicchi" by KAWAKAMI Mieko
© KAWAKAMI Mieko, 2013

This piece was published in the literary journal *Shincho* first in 2013,
and in 2014 it was included in the novel *Akogare*, which is a
combination of two stories: 'Ms Ice Sandwich' and 'Strawberry Jam
Minus Strawberry'

English translation © 2017 Louise Heal Kawai
First published by Pushkin Press in 2017
This edition first published in 2020

The publisher gratefully acknowledges the support of the British
Centre for Literary Translation and the Nippon Foundation

The publisher would like to thank David Karashima, Michael
Emmerich and Elmer Luke for their editorial work and support

9 8

ISBN 13: 978-1-78227-672-2

Designed and typeset by Tetragon, London
Printed and bound by Clays Ltd, Elcograf S.p.A.

www.pushkinpress.com

MS ICE
SANDWICH

TWO-HUNDRED-THIRTEEN to Florida, three-hundred-twenty to polite, three-hundred-eighty to church medicine, four-hundred-fifteen to choco skip, four-hundred-thirty to your forties, vegetable boots is always five-hundred. Five-hundred-twelve is a gravestone for rain; the big cat bench where all the girls like to hang out in the evenings is six-hundred-seven.

If someone speaks to me I lose count, so I keep my head down and try not to catch anyone's eye. Sometimes there's a crack in the white line I'm following, and sometimes it breaks off for a bit, but I keep my concentration, and the soles of my trainers land spot-on the line and I do it with a steady rhythm. Seven-hundred-thirty-one is souvenirs, eight-hundred-twenty, wait a minute, wait a minute, eight-hundred-eighty a famous writer, and nine-hundred-twelve a French person. At this point it's suddenly crowded, full of people, and bicycles are lined up like mechanical goats.

The automatic doors open and out pour people holding white plastic shopping bags stuffed with food. I guess they're on their way home. Most of them are grown-ups. One in five has bought those leeks with their green tops poking out, and the bags look like they're about to burst. Just as I'm thinking how most of the stuff they've bought is going to be put in their mouths, I'm surprised by people saying *hello, good evening* to me. I say it back. Then, careful not to bump into anyone, on to the potato zone, nine-hundred-thirty. And then always, without fail, it's nine-hundred-fifty exactly to Ms Ice Sandwich.

The cheapest sandwich you can buy there is the egg sandwich. There are two to a pack, but they're superthin, and I come every day, or every other day, to buy them. If Mum sends me to the supermarket, I can pay for my sandwich with her money, so I like to hang around the house hoping she'll ask me to go shopping for her, but sometimes I have to use my own pocket money. I get one hundred yen a day five times a week,

Monday to Friday, and I make sure I put half of it in my coin purse. My sandwich money. To tell the truth, I don't even like sandwiches that much; in fact, for meals I definitely like rice instead of bread, and for a snack it's much better to buy a big bag of crisps or something, and eat them really slowly one piece at a time, and anyway, I never really get that hungry. I get full after I've eaten about half of my school lunch, and that might be why I'm so skinny and I don't seem to be getting any taller. But I can't help it if I don't like what they serve. Mum got so worried she came to school and showed my teacher how skinny my arms were for a boy, but now that I think about it, that was ages ago, and it seems like she's forgotten all about it by now, or maybe she's just given up, or maybe the moment's passed, or that's what it feels like.

Around the train station, there's only the chemist's and the level crossing and the supermarket that are lit up at night. But to be honest there's not much there in the daytime either—this town is really just made up of houses, and the top floor of that two-storey supermarket is full of laundry detergent and buckets and dishes and toilet paper, all those things that's not food, and the meat and the vegetables and yogurt and fish and stuff is all on the ground floor, and everyone in the town comes here nearly every day to buy what they need. I watch Ms Ice Sandwich from the only door in and out of the supermarket; she's always standing behind a big round glass case, just to the left and a little bit behind the cash registers, with that look on her face that's like a mixture of surprise and boredom, as she's selling sandwiches and salads and bread and things like that.

"Ms Ice Sandwich" is a name I made up, of course. I thought of it the minute I first saw her. Ms Ice Sandwich's eyelids are always painted with a thick layer of a kind of electric blue, exactly the same colour as those hard ice lollies that have been sitting in our freezer since last summer. There's one more awesome thing about her—if you watch when she looks down, there's a sharp dark line above her eyes, as if when she closed her eyes, someone started to draw on two extra eyes with a felt-tip pen but stopped halfway. It's the coolest thing. And then when she looks straight at me, she has these enormous eyes which are so big I feel like I get swallowed up in them. They look exactly like the great big eyes of the dogs that I read about in a storybook long ago... What is the title of that book? Well, it's not only the title that I've forgotten, I can't even remember what happens in the story, but I do remember the faces of the dogs with their gigantic eyes; it must have been a children's picture book or something... Anyway, Ms Ice Sandwich has eyes just like those dogs do in that story, which has a soldier in it, and a castle, and there's a princess—*that* story. The dogs with the giant eyes run around like crazy everywhere. Where was it they came from? And then someone got married to someone else, or they didn't get married, I forget what the story was about.

The day I first saw Ms Ice Sandwich, I was with Mum, but when I said out loud in surprise, *Look at her eyes!*, Mum pretended not to hear me and started talking about something totally different, and it wasn't until we'd paid for our shopping and got completely outside the supermarket that she started in on me. *You have to stop that! You cannot say things like that out loud, she can hear you, it's rude.* Mum's face is awesome whenever she gets annoyed, if there was an animal that didn't know what being annoyed meant, then just one look at my mum's face and they'd get the idea. You could make a rubber stamp of Mum's face as a demo. I say, *Why can't I talk out loud about her eyes? They're huge, they're amazing!* Mum says, *It doesn't matter what they are, it's not proper to talk about other people's faces.* Me: *Why?* Her: *Because!* All the way home I keep asking

Mum *why*, but now she's busy playing with her mobile phone and just keeps nodding and saying *yeah* every so often. Well, I'm kind of getting used to her being like that these days, not paying attention to me, but the more we walk the more it bugs me, so I stop and say, *If video games make you stupid, then what do mobile phones do to you?* (This is me being real extreme to her.) She answers, *What?*, not stopping, *I'm not playing a game, I'm updating something. It's work. It's hot, can we walk faster?* And of course she hasn't taken her eyes off the screen for a second, madly pressing buttons, and keeps on walking.

Our house is the kind you can find anywhere around, one of those old brown houses made of wood with tiles on the roof, but last year, without warning, my mum suddenly had the entranceway and the room right next to it remodelled Western-style.

Mum stood there with a smile on her face, looking at the new section of the house that had been knocked to pieces one moment and then rebuilt the next. *I can't start up without my own salon*, she said, all happy, but if you ask me—and maybe I'm the only one who thinks this way—somehow the colours and the design don't go together, are all mixed up, like she's taken one of those little booths or stalls at an amusement park where you can buy snacks or stuff and stuck it in our house, it's just really, really weird. It was so much better before with nothing there, and now every time I come home, it's so embarrassing to have to look at that and it always makes me feel kind of bad.

Mum's into fortune telling and that kind of stuff, well, actually her job is something to do with that, but if you look too long at this new salon room that she's set up, your eyes start to hurt from the red carpet, and the foreign furniture, and then there's a computer, and she's hung little angels on the walls, and on the floor next to the door is a sculpture thing with a sparkly, powdery surface like a massive sugar cube with spikes coming out of it that look like swords that would really hurt if you sat on them by mistake. Well, her friends—or is it the people she works with?—or her customers?—anyway, these women come over and they talk on and on. But then sometimes, even though I know she has people over, a whole hour goes by with nobody saying a word, and I wonder what's going on, so I creep right up close to the door and put my ear against it, and then out of nowhere I hear a noise as if somebody's starting to cry... Anyway, I don't know exactly what Mum's doing in there, but sometimes she needs to talk to me about something and I get a chance to look at what's going on inside the room. There are all these little bottles lined up on the table and people are going around taking a sniff of this one and that one, and banging on this thing like a cooking pot that makes a loud donging sound, anyway, everything in the room—my mum and the other women and the things and the air and every single bit of it—it's very creepy. The full-on stink is terrible enough to give me a headache, and the donging pot has water in it, so there's this horrid low echo in my ears, and the women're all different people with different faces, but they all start looking the same and laughing the same way, and on their wrists they're all wearing different-coloured bands of things that look like pearls. They hold their hands out over the pot, they drink something, they turn over cards and decide whether there's a full moon that night or not... anyway this is how my mum spends most days—inviting people to come over to the house and they talk a lot.

But I know the truth—the reason we can live here like this is because of Grandma.

Grandma isn't my mum's mum. She's my dad's mum. He died when I was four years old. This house where I was born and I've lived all my life is Grandma's house, and although my dad died, or maybe it was because my dad died—I'm not sure—but anyway because Grandma would be all alone, me and Mum stayed on living in the house and taking care of her, and so it somehow became OK for Mum to use a little bit of Grandma's money and something called her pension, I think. Well, I guess now it's become OK for her to use it any way she wants.

Until recently, Grandma was really healthy, but one day, right after I started the second year at school, she couldn't walk properly any more, and then a little while later, she couldn't talk properly either, and then for the last two years, she hasn't been able to get out of bed. So I guess she has no idea that her house has been altered in such a weird way, and when I think of her I can't help feeling Mum did a really wrong and selfish thing, and I even start to get angry, but then I remember I'm just as guilty as her because I didn't tell Grandma what was happening, and when I think of this I get this feeling like regret or sadness bubbling up inside me and my heart begins to pound. Still, there are times I also think that it's probably better that my grandma never sees how messed up her house looks now, and I suppose that's why I haven't said anything to her. Anyway, I was sure I could make everybody at school laugh when I told them about all the weird changes in our house, but it turns out that Doo-Wop either has no taste whatsoever, or maybe he just doesn't have any interest in that kind of thing in the first place, and all he says is *Oh, you got more? More of what?* We haven't got more of anything, and that was the end of the conversation. Doo-Wop's still totally obsessed with how to get some password code for some video game that everyone else got fed up and bored with long ago, and he won't talk about anything but that game—not during calligraphy lessons, or at school, not even at the park after school. He isn't really fitting in with the rest of us any more, but I don't know if I should mention this to Doo-Wop, and then if I did decide to say something, how should I put it to him? And if I told him straight, then he might get annoyed and say all sorts of things back to me... I've been thinking about all kinds of stuff lately, about the money, and about Grandma... so seeing as tonight I'm not tired at all yet, I think I'll go to bed and stare up at the ceiling and think about it all, and then I start thinking, *What was it exactly that was what way?*, and somehow the swirls in the grain of the wood start to expand and contract and I begin to feel sleepy, and then my head and my chest fill up with some kind of fog and I can't seem to work this or that or anything out in my mind.

The day I went shopping with Mum and saw Ms Ice Sandwich for the first time was the first day of swimming lessons in the summer holiday. I was really tired—well, I'm always like that after swimming—but anyway I started going to see Ms Ice Sandwich by myself after that. I get back from the pool and do a bit of my homework first, then when Mum asks me to go shopping for her—or even if she doesn't—I walk there by my special system, calling out the right names at the right places, placing my feet on the white line at the edge of the road with total precision, all the way to Ms Ice Sandwich.

Ms Ice Sandwich has really short hair, her head looks just like an *onigiri* rice ball with a sheet of *nori* wrapped tightly around it. Of course she's got a nose and a mouth too, but all you notice when you see her are those eyes, then when afterwards you try to remember them, you know, what shape they are or what they looked like, you just can't picture them exactly. At first I hold Mum's shopping list in my right hand and pick up eggs and leeks and stuff and put them in the shopping basket. (What I want to know is why everyone has to buy leeks every single day—that stuff is tasteless!) And I'm trying to walk around the store as many times as possible, all the time glancing over at the sandwich counter, but when there aren't any customers, Ms Ice Sandwich stands back at the far end of the glass case, and I can't see her face. Then I wonder what I'm going to do now that I can't see those big eyes, and I hang around a bit, and suddenly it's like there's a flash of light right in the middle of my forehead, and I decide to go and stand in front of the glass case and buy a sandwich like it's normal, and I think what a cool plan I've come up with. I'm so nervous about making my first ever sandwich purchase, but then I manage to put a completely casual expression on my face, and somehow I do it. I buy a sandwich directly from Ms Ice Sandwich, and in the few seconds that it takes, I'm able to stare at Ms Ice Sandwich's great big eyes. And from really close up too.

Ms Ice Sandwich isn't friendly at all. When the customers come and stand in front of the glass case and stare at all the sandwiches and stuff inside it, she never bothers to say *Hello* or *Can I help you?* or *What can I do for you?* or any of those usual things that people who work in shops say. She never speaks to anyone unless they speak to her first. When a customer asks for something, she doesn't smile, she just stands there going *clack clack* with her silver pincers as she confirms the order: *This is the kind you want?* or *You want two, right?* Then she slips the sandwich into a bag without saying anything except how much it's going to cost. But the way she handles those pincers, everything's so quick and neat, it's so cool, in the blink of an eye—not one second more—the sandwich she's grabbed with the pincers has already disappeared into a plastic bag. I have no idea how she does it, and it doesn't matter what shape the sandwich is, long or round or normal, Ms Ice Sandwich always manages to slip it spot on, straight into the bag. I could stand there all day and watch her do that, but to be honest, for me it's Ms Ice Sandwich's eyes that I really want to look at, and while she's doing all that stuff with the pincers and sandwiches and bags, she's looking downwards, and so that whenever she has customers, the entire time I can gaze at Ms Ice Sandwich's ice-blue eyelids with their clean, dark line.

I concentrate on Ms Ice Sandwich and I don't ever want my turn to come. I hardly blink. Then when she finally takes my money and gives me the change and her eyelids turn upwards and I can see those great big eyes again, without any warning that squishy, yellowy, orangey stuff inside my head becomes extra bright, then that hollow place right under my chin, above my collarbone, feels like it's being squeezed really tightly. It's like that feeling you get when you swallow rice without chewing it properly first. And that lump begins to move from my throat and travel slowly, slowly all the way downwards, until it ends up in a bigger place, a kind of open, roomy space—a place soft like a rabbit's ear. And with every breath I take, it begins to grow, it gets longer and wider. I've never seen the middle of the ocean or the edge of the sky, but maybe the kind of breeze that blows in those places now comes blowing in out of nowhere and I feel it wrapped around me. Like when you're holding a cat and you touch its soft belly. Or sticking your finger in a jar of jam and stirring, then slowly sinking in all the rest of your fingers. Or licking the sweet condensed milk at the bottom of your bowl of strawberries. Or when a blanket brushes the top of your feet. Or when butter turns transparent when it melts over your pancakes. As I stand gazing at Ms Ice Sandwich, all of these things are happening to me, one on top of the other, right there in my rabbit's ear.

When I reach out to get my order from Ms Ice Sandwich, the air suddenly goes cold. She's still turned in my direction, but her eyes have shifted to the next customer, and that magical breeze stops blowing. The blanket is ripped away, the condensed milk dries up, the cat runs off, and finally the rabbit's ear droops. There's nothing to do but to walk slowly towards the doors, head down, eyes fixed on the toes of my trainers. I glance up once I'm outside, but there's nothing to see. I realize it's the same old place in this same old town with all its houses squashed together. The stuffy summer evening air rises up from the ground, and it's suddenly difficult to breathe. The place in my chest where I keep the air gets tighter and tighter, and I don't know exactly what it is, but I do know that I'm going to find out sometime that somewhere in this town there's something bad, and that those long shadows creeping up in the dark have come to tell me about it. Afraid of being caught by the shadows, I hurry home, my plastic sandwich bag swinging from my hand, and then the next day, I go to the supermarket again, and just like before I stare at Ms Ice Sandwich's awesome eyes, which gives me a brand-new, really happy feeling. I do the same thing every day and that's how I end up spending the whole summer filling myself with Ms Ice Sandwich's eyes (and my stomach with her sandwiches).

ON THE THURSDAY right after the autumn school term starts, there are only morning classes, and the afternoon is emergency evacuation training for when in case there's an earthquake or something, which means we have to gather in our walking groups and go home together that way. Everyone in a walking group is in different classes and different school years (we're put in groups by how close our homes are to each other), so that the things everyone wants to talk about, and how fast they walk, and what they do when they're walking are all over the place, so it takes about twice the time it usually does to get home.

The sixth graders are big and a little bit scary, the fifth graders act all important and sometimes get too rough; the first graders are little, which I guess is to be expected, but they're kind of unsteady on their feet like nursery-school kids, and the square backpacks they're wearing are so big on them it looks like they're about to fall over backwards any moment. The second graders walk with their mouths open and you can't tell what they're thinking, but they look like they're kind of grinning, and there's one third grader who's really noisy, she never stops singing this song she made up. And out of this strange bunch of kids walking home together, it's only us fourth graders who are walking normally. Actually, I'm not sure what it means to walk normally, which is what I was just thinking about when something hits me on the back of my head and I nearly fall on my face. I'm shocked, and then I realize that someone's done a *nevermore* on me and I turn back to see Tutti—the only person in the walking group from the same class as me.

"Nevermore!"

She's about to hit me on the head a second time, so I run to the front of the line to get away. I can't remember exactly when it got started, but if you see a crow you're allowed to hit the person nearest to you on top of the head as hard as you like, and it's not really a game or even much fun, so I don't know what you'd call it, but anyway it's this stupid pact that we made, supposedly, and it's not even just my class, it's been a thing for ages throughout the whole school, and I have no idea why. The rule is that you have to shout out *nevermore*, and the first person to say it is the one who gets to hit somebody. It's crazy. And this so-called game or whatever, which at some point got named Nevermore, is what Tutti has just done to me, even though I never heard her say it.

"Nevermore!"

"You can't keep saying it over and over."

"I'm not just saying it over and over. There's another crow now."

So she hits me over the head again, and I have to fix my hat, which has fallen to one side over my eye, then I keep on walking, ignoring Tutti who keeps chanting *nevermore, nevermore*, and trying to hit me again.

One lunchtime, soon after all the classes were reshuffled, Tutti thought she could get away with secretly farting in the classroom, but she was really unlucky because there was either a misfire or an accident or whatever you call it, but she ended up making this huge noise and everyone knew she'd farted, and worse, there was a big commotion because somehow her fart had that exact stinky, overripe smell that strawberries have when they're in a plastic box in the fridge, and suddenly the word Tutti-Frutti popped into my head, and without meaning to, I blurted it out. Everyone stopped and stared at me, and for a moment the whole room went dead quiet, and then everyone started shouting and laughing, and that was how Tutti got named Tutti. (By the way, Doo-Wop got his name the same way—from the sound of his fart. It's terrible if you're ever unlucky enough to fart at school.) For quite a while after that, Tutti acted like she had a big grudge against me, whenever our eyes met she glared at me like a mad dog, but it wasn't long before she got used to it, and it became totally natural for everyone to call her Tutti, even the teacher was calling her Tutti, and by the time the end of spring term came around, no one remembered that the name had anything to do with her farting, and she was just Tutti. One day, quite a long time after the naming incident, I found myself alone with her and I said, *I'm really sorry, I feel bad about giving you your name*, but after a little bit, Tutti looked me in the eyes and said *Oh well, never mind*. And then she said how the name Tutti-Frutti made her seem foreign and different and that maybe she would try dyeing her hair blonde, and then she laughed *hahaha*.

For a while, I was hoping that she really would dye her hair blonde, but she never did. She kept on coming to school with her usual black hair in the same bob cut. Actually there's a group of three girls in my class who dress in a way so that they stand out, and they dance together, but by dance I mean it's not just playing around mimicking stuff in girls' anime or what idol bands do, they do like serious dance. When other kids are going to a cram school after regular school, they go three times a week to a proper dance school, it's somewhere far away that has a specialist instructor, and they sometimes have recitals and competitions and stuff. Those girls don't fit in with other girls in our class, but not in the way Doo-Wop doesn't fit in; all the girls in the class kind of look up to them—that kind of different. During recess, they're hardly ever in the classroom (they're in the toilets or the sixth-grade building—even though they're not supposed to be). Doo-Wop and I never talk to these girls. It's like there's a barrier of barbed wire or something, except it's invisible, that keeps us away from them. Well, it's not as if we really have anything to say to them... The other day when we had to make a newspaper, we ended up in the same group, and they spent the whole time just talking to each other and putting fancy stickers on their notebooks, and then running off to the toilet maybe to look at themselves in the mirror; they didn't contribute at all to the newspaper, but they're not the sort of kids you can tell off for stuff like that, they're too stuck-up, you know, kind of hard to get along with. The one girl who's kind of their leader has her hair dyed almost completely blonde and it's actually a pretty nice colour. But for some reason, I'm thinking how that blonde colour would look even prettier on Tutti. And so I'm always thinking how if Tutti dyed her hair blonde, it would be awesome, though I don't know why I like the idea of it, but that's how I feel. On the other hand, Tutti, no matter what she says, has had the same black hair and the exact same haircut since she was in first grade.

These days, even though it's not Valentine's Day or anything, the kids in class have been talking about who they like, and who likes who, and it all makes me feel kind of weird. Girls especially like talking about that kind of thing and they're always making a big fuss about it. I don't get how they can go on and on about all that stuff, it's a mystery to me. I mean who likes who and all that, stuff about other people, you never know if it's true or made-up, a lie—it's all just gossip, I mean it's not really interesting or fun at all, but there are even some boys who're into talking about that stuff now, even though only last year they said they hated it. I don't understand what's happened to *them*. But whenever the kids in the class start gossiping like this, I notice Tutti always sneaks back to her seat and starts writing something in her notebook, and I like that about her; she's not annoying like most girls, she's kind of cool really... and she's easy to talk to too.

On top of that, Tutti has a really unusual hobby. I heard that one of the rooms in her house is stuffed floor to ceiling with piles of movies, or rather DVDs, probably her dad's, anyway they watch them all the time, and Tutti says they're going to watch every single one of them, starting at one end of the room and working through to the other end. But these aren't the kind of movies that you go and watch at the cinema during New Year's or in the summer, you know, the usual movies for kids—anime and things like that. I think some of them are in English, and they have subtitles, anyway movies from foreign countries, and one day before school let out for summer we were walking home from school and Tutti was telling me about those movies, and then she says, *What do you do after school?*, but I didn't have an answer, I didn't know. (Well, if she asked me now, I could tell her that I go to the supermarket to see Ms Ice Sandwich—or maybe I wouldn't tell her—but back then I didn't use to do anything special.) So I decide, instead of trying to answer, I would just ask Tutti a question of my own. Yeah, about movies... *Isn't it boring to just sit and watch a whole movie all the way through?* I say, and Tutti says, *It's really fun*, and for a moment her eyes get this kind of twinkly light in them, and I see that black pupils can seem kind of white when they sparkle. And then Tutti says, *Me and my dad have movie night once a week, it's kind of like a family tradition, and you know, you want to come over sometime and watch with us? Your house is near mine, and we eat loads of popcorn and stuff,* and then she went home. I thought that didn't sound too bad, but I'd sometimes seen Tutti's dad at holiday events or pounding *mochi* at New Year's, and for some reason I didn't like talking to him, but then soon after that it was summer and that's as far as me and Tutti got to talking about movie night.

MONDAYS AND THURSDAYS, a home-helper comes to our house to give Grandma a bath and a massage. After school on days when I don't have calligraphy lessons or when it's raining, or between the time I come home from playing in the park and dinner time, I always go and sit in Grandma's bedroom and do my homework or read a book, and on Mondays and Thursdays she always looks like she's smiling a little bit, and she looks kind of happy. Of course, she can't talk at all, but I'm sure she understands what I'm saying when I talk to her, because the corners of her eyes and her mouth move slightly and I'm sure she's giving me a sign that she's listening, and sometimes she even nods her head, for sure.

On that subject, there used to be time a while ago when I was interested in what part of a person's face tells you whether they're sad or happy, and there's even a saying that the eyes speak like the mouth does, but different of course, so I thought that the eyes were supposed to hold some kind of secret, but that turned out to be false, because according to the results of my experiments it turns out that eyes don't have those special powers at all. When I look in the mirror and cover my mouth and eyebrows with my hands, so that all I can see are my eyes, I can't tell what emotion I'm feeling at all. I try pulling all sorts of faces but you can't tell what kind of face it is from the eyes alone. My conclusion is that when it comes to the face, emotions are seventy per cent from the eyebrows and thirty per cent from the mouth. In the case of my grandma, she doesn't have eyebrows any more, and no teeth either, and her mouth which is always a little bit open looks kind of like a dark little hole, but even so, I'm not sure how, I can always tell what Grandma is thinking. I look at the pattern of wrinkles on her face and the movement of her cheek-bones and stare hard into her eyes, and these things reveal to me what Grandma is feeling. I don't know how it is that I can tell but I do.

The only people in the whole world who know about Ms Ice Sandwich are me and Grandma. Whenever Mum goes into her salon and it doesn't look like she's going to be coming out anytime soon, or whenever all those ladies are over, I tell Grandma about Ms Ice Sandwich. And sometimes I sit at the low table in her room, which is actually a *kotatsu* table without the quilt covering, and draw pictures of Ms Ice Sandwich. I start by drawing the outline of her face, then the fringe part of her hair. Next, I draw a kind of nose. Then her mouth. And last of all, after I draw her two huge eyes, I colour the eyelids in bright blue, and right away it looks just like her, and I feel very pleased with myself and I make the noise *mmm*, like I'm satisfied. Then I stand up and step backwards so I can look at Ms Ice Sandwich from a little distance. The more you look at the drawing from this distance, the more it looks almost exactly like her. But I think of this as just a practice drawing, what you call a sketch. One day I want to paint a real picture of Ms Ice Sandwich. Use electric ice-blue paint and draw those enormous, totally awesome eyes. And her hard-working silver pincers. And her face that never smiles. Grandma mostly just lies there silently listening, but sometimes it's like she smiles or nods. And this makes me happy, so I talk to Grandma about all kinds of things.

On the other hand, there isn't really anything that I can talk about with my mum. We hardly ever eat dinner at the same time, because Mum doesn't really eat dinner (and by the way she doesn't even believe in having a microwave oven in our house). While I'm in the kitchen eating the dinner Mum has made me, she's in Grandma's room feeding her, and then after that we take turns having a bath, and finally right before we go to sleep on our futon arranged next to each other's, we get to talk a little bit, and it's been like that between us for a long time.

Mum told me a while back that the reason she doesn't eat dinner is that the sweet taste of food is harmful to her spirit. When she doesn't eat, her spirit has a chance to wash away its stains, kind of like moving to a higher level. Mum says all human beings have these things called spirit, and human beings can be divided into groups according to their spirit level; it's kind of like they have a report card with number grades on it that tell you what level their spirit's at, and Mum says when she meets somebody, just by doing one simple thing, she can tell right away, like a flash of light or something, the number that is their spirit level. What she does is, she checks the position and movement of the stars in the universe and she can tell people who are suffering from troubles in this world all about what is in their souls, and helps them go and live a happy life, and that's her mission in life, she says. At about that point, I get it mixed up in my head and can't follow what Mum is explaining to me, but that is the stuff that we talk about every night before we go to sleep. Mum likes to say, *If I'm in a good mood and having fun, then it's really good for the whole family, if I'm happy then you're happy too, right?* She's always saying that, and I think, well, I suppose that's true, but I can't help feeling that sometimes maybe it'd be nice to talk about something else besides Mum's work or Mum's happiness. So the other night before we went to sleep I said to her, *You know that story that has the dogs with the giant eyes? You used to read it to me when I was little? The one with the big dogs that are running?* And Mum says, *Where are they running to?* And I say, *I don't know but I'm sure it was in a foreign country.*

Mum, who's sitting on her futon meditating as usual, opens her eyes and stares up into space for a while, it looks like she's thinking quite hard about this. *Hmm, I don't remember that one.* And I say, *OK, but if you remember could you tell me the name of the story about the dogs, you know, with the really humungous eyes...* And then I must have fallen asleep without realizing it, and when deep in the middle of the night I open my eyes and look at the futon next to me, Mum isn't there.

HOW CAN SOMEONE yell like from deep down in their throat at someone they don't even know? So loud the air starts to shake? What is it with some grown-ups whose whole body, their back, their forehead, their eyes, their hands get puffed up so much, until they explode? Just thinking about it makes me cringe. How could someone act so weird?

It happened on Monday, the busiest evening of the week at the supermarket. I was standing right behind this man, waiting my turn, in front of Ms Ice Sandwich's glass case, watching her every move. Ms Ice Sandwich's shop isn't so popular that you always have to queue, but this day customers were lined up past the end of the glass case, beyond the meat counter, all the way to the eggs. The man looked ordinary and normal, like the kind of guy—there are loads of them around here—who you see out walking his dog, that kind of person. He was wearing a brown polo shirt and shorts and black sandals, and from what I could see, he might have been losing some hair on the top of his head. He was waiting for his turn in the queue just like everybody else as the sandwiches were sliding into their plastic bags, guided by Ms Ice Sandwich's silver pincers. One by one the customers were passing in front of her after being handed a bag of whatever they'd bought.

Suddenly a man started yelling. I knew that it was the man in front of me who was yelling because I was right there next to him, but it happened without any warning and I couldn't figure out who he could be yelling at. My heart began to go *boom boom boom* so loud that I was sure everyone around me could hear it and my pulse took over my whole body, and I was trembling like jelly. I started gripping the edge of my trouser pockets and took a couple of steps backwards.

It's Ms Ice Sandwich the man is yelling at. For a second there's a buzz of voices and then everything goes quiet, and the neat queue dissolves and everyone's crowding around the man and Ms Ice Sandwich, but instead of stopping yelling, the man gets louder and louder, his face turning purple, and I keep thinking he's going to jump over the glass case or smash his fist down on it or something, he's in such a state, shaking his finger at Ms Ice Sandwich, spit flying. What happened? I was right behind him, I didn't see anything. It looks like everyone else has no idea either, they've all got very shocked expressions on their faces, watching the man. Two women next to me are so scared they're grabbing hold of each other—they might be more freaked out than me.

The man doesn't stop raving. And slowly I begin to figure out what he's yelling about, he doesn't like Ms Ice Sandwich's *attitude*. He's going on about *the service industry* and *it's a disgrace, your behaviour* and *answer me, dammit, say something!* and *why should I bother talking to you, go get your manager right away* and *wait, you should be responsible, I want to hear it from you, explain yourself*, getting more and more worked up by the sound of his own voice, which is getting louder and louder.

And what does Ms Ice Sandwich do during all of this? She stands there, doesn't say a word, stares at the man with her head to one side, her chin sticking out, arms folded—pincers in hand—she never moves a muscle. Those amazing ice-blue eyes, they aren't exactly glaring at the man, just fixing him with a stare. She is flat like a picture. But her colours are even more vivid, more than usual, she looks exactly how a painting of

Ms Ice Sandwich would look. Isn't she afraid? She is the target of this man who's losing it, who's right in front of her, and she is just standing completely still, staring at him, not showing any fear. Me, right next to the action, I am scared out of my mind, how can Ms Ice Sandwich just stay there like that? She must have been standing on something on the other side of the glass case, a platform maybe, because Ms Ice Sandwich looks taller, like she's looking down on the man, who is still ranting.

Before long, the door behind the fish counter swings open and a man in a suit, maybe someone important, maybe the supermarket manager, comes out, and the man who was yelling is now mumbling and complaining, but not yelling any more, and everyone starts to go about their own business again. The store's music has probably been playing the whole time but I can hear it now. I thought the man had pretty much calmed down but now he starts up again, turning his anger on the manager, which it seems the man in the suit is, and the manager has this worried look on his face and is bowing and apologizing over and over.

While this was going on, I found myself standing in front of the eggs, where I started to notice that next to me there is someone, a grown-up I knew, but didn't know, well, kind of knew from somewhere, and he noticed me too. It was Tutti's dad. His hair was sort of long, like a girl's, and all messy, and he was wearing glasses and a raggedy old T-shirt and shorts, and he was holding a yellow wallet. *What a fool, making a scene like that*, he said with a smile. I didn't feel like smiling back, so I didn't and just kept quiet. Then he said, *Stress... that's the only excuse... zero manners... none... at all*, and grinned again, but I couldn't tell if he was talking to himself or to me. Anyway that was the kind of thing he was muttering, that's right, Tutti's dad always had that strange way of talking with all those pauses between his words, and when he spoke to you, you never knew what to say back to him, and anyway there wasn't really any way to know the timing of when to say *you're right* and *I know* and stuff like that, so I didn't say anything. The two of us stood for a while there in front of the eggs without speaking. And then Tutti's dad reached down and picked up a carton of eggs and said, *Do you like eggs?* I shook my head as hard as I could.

Pulling myself together, I left Tutti's dad by the eggs and went back to Ms Ice Sandwich's glass case. While all the fuss was calming down, a whole new queue had formed, and I took my place at the end of it. After about ten minutes, my turn finally came, but then, again suddenly, there's this hoarse shouting, *You still need to apologize!* from somewhere. I automatically turn my head. The man's almost at the front door of the supermarket but it's like he can't give it up and had to have the last word before he left.

Ms Ice Sandwich just stands where she is, barely acknowledging the man, though she might have laughed a little. *Uh-oh*, I think, as in a flash the man comes storming back to the glass case, the manager chasing after him. *Is she taking the piss?* the man screams at the manager, then he looks square at Ms Ice Sandwich—speaking loudly and clearly, *Listen to me, you ugly cow. I come here every day to buy my groceries, and every day I have to see your painted monster face. Butt-ugly females like you, you think you're better than anybody else with your facial reconstruction crap. You shouldn't even be allowed out in public.* That's what the man said to her.

BACK AT HOME that night, the scene replayed over and over, the yelling, the terrified women, the music that seemed to stop and then start up again, the tension in the air, everything, like live action. I couldn't fall asleep, I tried, I couldn't. I kept seeing Ms Ice Sandwich standing there, staring at the man, daring him.

The next morning I couldn't wait to get to school. I figured Tutti would know about what happened from her dad and we could talk and she could tell me what she thought. I get to school way early and wait in the classroom for Tutti, who gets there at the usual time. I rush over and I say, *Hey, I met your dad yesterday.* But she doesn't say, *Oh yeah, he told me about the stuff at the supermarket,* or anything like that, she just says, *Oh yeah?* with a kind of blank look on her face. And I say, *Yeah,* but then I don't know how to go about starting to tell her the story, and she doesn't ask me questions, so I just say, *Yeah* one more time and nod, *That's right,* and I don't even know why I'm saying what I'm saying, and I notice I'm laughing even though there's nothing funny. Tutti's looking at me like she doesn't have a clue, and I stand there a few moments before heading over to my own desk to put down my backpack and my gym bag. I start to pretend there's nothing wrong, and walk over to the blackboard and, even though it's not my turn to be classroom monitor today, I begin cleaning the board and laying out the chalk neatly, before going back and sitting down.

The whole day I don't really feel like myself (though, to tell the truth, I don't really know what it means to feel like myself), and today is the worst day of the week for lessons, because it's Tuesday, and we have Maths, followed by Science, and then PE, and then after it in fourth period, Music. I can't believe whoever made that schedule: they know nothing about kids and how they feel through the day, what were they thinking, putting things in that order? I suppose it's made by teachers to suit the teachers, but I have to admit, although I have the perfect schedule in my head, I'm pretty sure it doesn't exist anywhere on this earth, so I know there's no point in blaming everything on Tuesday, but now that I think about it, at least after lunch there's Art class, which makes the day bearable. I like Art. We don't even have to stand up and bow when the bell goes off for class; I can just go over and collect my art project and work on it at my own pace over several weeks and draw whatever I like, and I wish that every day's schedule could be made up of Tuesday afternoons. I'm absolutely serious about this.

Last week I finished sketching so finally I'm up to the next step, which is colouring it in with paint, which I'm a little nervous about. If I make a mistake, I can paint over it, but if I do that too much, it weakens the paper. I have to take extra care when I use black. Black in a painting looks really cool, but if you make a mistake there's no way to go back and fix it. After putting bluish-green and a little bit of white on my palette, I glance over at Tutti, and she's just picked up her water container and is going to fill it. I pick up my own container and follow her out of the classroom.

"Hey," I say, standing next to her, slowly filling the different compartments under the tap, "are you starting on the painting today?"

"Yep," she answers, glancing up at me.

"What are you painting?"

"A gunfight."

"Huh?" For a moment, I thought I heard her say the word *gun* so I ask her again, "What are you painting?"

"I'm painting a gunfight."

I wasn't wrong, she did say *gun*, so now I ask her another question, a little excited, "What kind of gunfight?"

"They shoot each other," said Tutti, as if it was the most normal thing in the world. "What are you painting?"

"I'm... well... scenery."

"Huh."

The conversation gets interrupted for a moment as she balances her water container on the palms of her hands. We both set off very slowly and carefully back to the classroom, trying not to spill any water.

"Why are you painting a gunfight?" I ask casually.

"Why are you painting scenery?" she answers.

"Well," I say, thinking for a moment. "Maybe because it's beautiful?"

Tutti looks me in the eye for a second and then just says *huh*, again, with a kind of bored expression on her face, and goes back to her desk.

A kind of film has begun to form over the top of my bluish-green and white paints, so I dip my small paint-brush in the water and gently try to brush it away, then the colours start to dissolve and bleed. It looks like the paints trapped underneath the film are trying to escape, and as I press down on the tip of my brush, trying not to break the film, I have this gloomy feeling in my heart. It's because of the conversation I just had with Tutti. I shouldn't have told her that was my reason for painting scenery, I mean I should have thought about it more so that I could explain it properly to her. And I just said *scenery* off the top of my head without thinking, but is it really scenery that I'm painting? Up until last week, I was really concentrating on drawing the glass windows of a greenhouse and all the leaves on the olive tree next to it. I want to paint all the different colours on the surface of the glass that change with the light, and I want to use a thick layer of bluish-green paint to show how thick and strong the olive leaves look, and so that's why I chose those two things to paint. Now that I think about it that's not really scenery, or anything else. At least I could have told Tutti all this stuff that's in my head right now. Or maybe not. Maybe that's not it at all. To start with, my question *Why are you painting a gunfight?* wasn't a good one. It was probably too nosy, and it was none of my business. Nobody should have to explain what they choose to paint and how they feel about painting it. And this makes my heart turn one shade darker. I wonder if I'll get the chance to apologize to Tutti, or at least explain. Probably not. This whole thing will probably just fade away. People always forget about these little things, but I believe that each one stays somewhere deep in everyone's heart, and without noticing it they grow and harden, until one day they cause something terrible to happen. And as I'm thinking about this, I get depressed, and now all of these things that I thought I'd done such a good job of drawing begin to fade and grow dull—even though I haven't even started painting them yet.

Except for my mood, the whole classroom is bright and noisy right now. Art is different from all the other lessons, and for some reason this kind of atmosphere is OK. The three dance girls are the worst, they're barely even holding their paintbrushes, and they're sitting with all their desks pushed together, and they're talking about something completely different from painting, loudly, and it must be something really funny because they keep on shrieking with laughter. I'm thinking how annoying they are, but I don't tell them off or anything—well, to tell the truth I'm kind of scared to. So I decide to pretend the three girls don't even exist, and to pay attention to the tiny leaves in front of me, and take my brush and dab them with bluish-green paint. This moment, this feeling. When you first look at it, the surface of the drawing paper looks totally flat, but if you look carefully there are bumps and pits in the surface. Like the bumpy, rocky surface of a mountain. Coloured rain pours down on it, and before you realize it, the surface has completely changed. I pick up my brush, which I've soaked in this rain, take a slight breath, and swallow.

"Yes, I know! The sandwich lady. I know who you mean. She's such a freak."

I'm leaning forward over my painting, about to touch the tip of the brush to it when I hear a voice saying the word *sandwich*. I immediately turn to look and it's the blonde-haired girl and she's shaking her head and laughing and saying, *No way!* My chest gets all hot at the word *sandwich*, and for a moment I can't move. Then all the nerves in my body are focused in my ears so I don't miss the rest of the conversation, and my hand grips the paintbrush really tightly. *Sandwich... The sandwich lady...* Who are they talking about?

"You know I always wonder how they can make a mistake like that these days. It's really scary."

"Yeah, but she's got to be brave. Think about it, she's going to look like that for the rest of her life."

"You know, ever since she took over, I haven't bought anything there."

"Me neither. I can't even look at her."

"Right. So creepy!"

"She looks like some kind of monster."

"Her hair's weird too. But her eyes are the worst."

"Her nose is kind of messed up as well. When you end up looking like that—well, there's no way she's ever going to get married, no way she's ever going to be able to do anything. It's like her life's over. She's a freak."

"Right. You know, if it was me..."

"What would you do?"

"Er, hello? I'd die of course."

Shrieks of laughter again.

I stand there, paintbrush in hand, waiting for whatever they're going to say next. But their talk seems to disappear along with their laughter, all swallowed up by the general noise of the classroom, but long after I stop hearing their voices, my heart is still pounding. They had to be talking about Ms Ice Sandwich, which I never imagined people would do, for some reason. And worst of all, it wasn't nice at all, it was all totally mean, and I remember the stuff that angry man said yesterday before he walked out of the supermarket, and I picture Ms Ice Sandwich's face. Ms Ice Sandwich with her big eyes and her ice-blue eyelids. I wonder for a while if I dare go over to the three girls and very casually get them to keep talking about her, but in the end I don't do it.

I still feel depressed after I get home. Of course I don't feel like doing any homework. Whenever I feel this way, I sit at the table in Grandma's room and try to write a list of what's on my mind. And then it feels as if the stuff that I don't understand, everything's that's too foggy, turns into words and leaves my body.

One: Everybody is saying bad things about Ms Ice Sandwich. And somehow it's all about Ms Ice Sandwich's face. Two: I heard them say it, but I couldn't bring myself to speak up. And this happened twice.

What did they mean by *mistake*? And what is *facial reconstruction*? I mean I kind of know what plastic surgery is, but I never would have guessed in a million years that there might be someone who had that done living so close, the words plastic surgery seem like something very far away from me. I don't really understand, but it's like they're saying that Ms Ice Sandwich has had this plastic surgery done, and somehow it failed. So Ms Ice Sandwich's face that I look at almost every day was made by plastic surgery. That's not Ms Ice Sandwich's real face? And if it's not, why did she do plastic surgery? Was there some reason why she had to change her face? But I can't imagine what that reason might be. And does this mean that anybody can have plastic surgery? And then if Ms Ice Sandwich's face was made by plastic surgery, how did those three girls and the angry man from yesterday know that? And they didn't just know that she had surgery, they were saying that it failed. What does failed plastic surgery mean? One of the girls said that if it was her, she'd die. And that Ms Ice Sandwich would never be able to get married, and that her life was over. They definitely said that. But why would they say that about Ms Ice Sandwich?

All my thoughts are getting more and more tangled up inside my head, so I go into the kitchen and get a glass of water and drink it down in one gulp.

When I get back to Grandma's room, I can tell from her breathing that she's asleep. It's weird but although I know she's been there lying in the exact same position the whole time, it feels as if I'm looking at her for the first time. The little bit of golden sun that shines through the *shoji* screens on the window lights up the white areas of Grandma's quilt, making a faint shadow of leaves, and each time the wind blows outside, the shadow pattern of leaves shakes a little bit. I go over to Grandma and I hold my breath for a moment. The room goes very quiet.

I think maybe Grandma's going to die soon, and then she won't be here any more. Sometimes when I find myself starting to think that way, I immediately try to stop it, but now I feel the thought slowly creeping out again. I picture a dent in the pillow where her head used to be and I squeeze my eyes tight for a moment. Grandma is sleeping. Peacefully. Her mouth is slightly open, she's making little breathing noises. Grandma's who's asleep and Grandma who's going to die. Are these the same Grandma?

I stare at sleeping Grandma's face and remember a photo I have of me on a swing with her when she wasn't so skinny and was much more healthy. Her loud laugh. The light purple sweater without sleeves that she always used to wear. Her hair long and tied back. Those Grandmas and this Grandma. The Grandmas I have in my head and the Grandma lying here with her eyes closed, quietly sleeping. Which is the real Grandma? The Grandma who used to pick me up from nursery school? The Grandma who made me her special veggie meatballs? Breakfast-time Grandma when she dipped her bread in coffee before eating it? Gentle Grandma who, whenever Mum scolded me and pushed me away, would sit next to me and let me talk? When Grandma goes away from this earth, where will she go? It's not happened yet, but I'm thinking about it now because I know that one day it's definitely, for sure, going to happen. And when I think about it, the air inside my chest gets heavier and heavier and it feels as if there's no escape. Grandma's still here, it's not like she's already died or anything, so why do I keep thinking this way?

"Hey, Grandma," I say quietly. Grandma doesn't wake up but I keep on talking.

"Today in Art I started painting in the colours."

My voice comes out really tiny and weak. I try to distract attention from it by fiddling with the edge of her quilt.

"And there's a rumour going around about Ms Ice Sandwich, I heard it today. You remember Ms Ice Sandwich? But this isn't the usual stuff I tell you, this is a bad thing. About her face and whatever."

But then I find that I can't say any more and I stop talking. It's silent in the room, like time has just stopped, but after a bit I can hear a bird chirping. It feels like it's coming from so close by that I spin around to check, but there are no birds anywhere.

"YOU MET MY DAD the other day."

When Tutti comes over and says that to me, I'm crouching down pulling on the broken end of my shoelace so that I can tie it, and I'm really trying to concentrate. She's standing behind me, and when I look up fast, it's at a weird angle and my neck makes this snapping noise. It hurts a little.

"Yes, I met him," I say, getting up. "Last week. Monday last week."

"So you said you're going to come and watch a movie?"

I don't remember saying anything like that. I'm about to say, *No, I didn't say that*, but Tutti talks first.

"My dad says on Friday night. Can you come?"

"Maybe. I have to ask. What movie?"

"It's already decided."

"OK. You said night. What time does night mean?"

"Obviously night means all of the time after you've eaten dinner," says Tutti with a face that says she can't believe I don't know that already.

"But I don't think I can come for all of the night."

"I don't mean *stay* all night. You asked me what night means. I just told you the meaning of night. That's all," says Tutti, sounding a little annoyed.

"Oh," I say.

"I mean we should spend part of the night watching a movie," she says, back to her usual grinning face. "After you eat dinner at home, come over. We're not going to do anything else. Just watch a movie."

After dinner on Friday, there's going to be a movie watching at Tutti's house. Can I go? I ask Mum. Her: *What time?* Me: *After dinner.* Her: *You can go as long as you don't stay too late.* Me: *OK.* And then, even though she doesn't ask me anything else, I add, for no particular reason, *It's me and Doo-Wop.* Her: *OK, I think I have their telephone number, but could you get it from them just in case, and let me know?* she asks, looking at the screen of her mobile phone. I don't know how I'm supposed to be able to find out anything right now, but she sits there staring at the screen and doesn't look up, and then finally says, *It's work. Something's come up. Go take a bath.* And she smiles.

In bed I close my eyes and think about how long it's been since I went to see Ms Ice Sandwich. Well, to tell the truth, these days before I go to sleep I've been thinking about nothing else, so I don't really need to try to count how long it's been, because I already know, but still I count one more time from the beginning, and today makes exactly one week. If I don't go tomorrow, it's going to be eight days that I haven't seen Ms Ice Sandwich. Eight whole days. Compared to the whole summer when I saw Ms Ice Sandwich almost every day. I sigh, feeling funny inside.

All the time when I'm walking, eating lunch at school, staring at the toes of my shoes, anywhere I go, I've been wondering why I stopped going to see Ms Ice Sandwich. And in my usual way, I've tried to write it down. What I've managed to figure out is it's partly because of that day in the classroom when I overheard those girls talking about her. After that whenever I thought about going to the supermarket and seeing Ms Ice Sandwich's face, it's not that I was afraid exactly, and I don't really know why, but the feeling of happiness that I used to feel when I saw her, I kind of know that I won't feel it again. Ever since, I've had this feeling of something strange pulling me back, and I didn't go to see her the next day, or the day after that. Even so, Ms Ice Sandwich's face is still really clear in my mind, I don't even have to try to remember, because those enormous eyes are always there, and I can still stare at those big, electric ice-blue eyelids. On nights like this I sit at the *kotatsu* table in Grandma's room and draw Ms Ice Sandwich's face in my sketchbook. In real life, our eyes never met—not once—but my drawing somehow has always her standing some place and looking right at me.

On Friday night, I take two bags of popcorn and head over to Tutti's house. It's the first time for me ever to go to a girl's house, and when I bend down to unlace my shoes, the back of my neck gets a bit hot. Tutti takes me into the living room, which has a sofa and smells of curry. I want to tell her I've just had curry for dinner too, but I can't find the right moment and I end up not saying anything.

"Let's start watching."

Besides a TV screen there's a bookshelf and a piano with a dust cover over it and a fish tank (I can't see any fish in it though) and a cabinet against the wall, and all over the carpet, which is a kind of dark cream colour, are piles of magazines and books. There's a tall Christmas tree standing in the corner, a silver star at the top leaning to one side. I recognize Tutti's lunch bag hanging on one of the lower branches.

Beyond, in the kitchen, wearing fuzzy blue slippers that look like mops, I see Tutti's dad; he waves a hand in my direction, and then brings us a soft drink.

"OK. Let's get started."

Tutti puts a DVD into the machine and clicks off the living-room lights. She squeezes into the middle of the short sofa with me on the right and her dad on the left, and we sit for a few moments silently staring at the dark screen.

It's a foreign movie with the title of *Heat*. The story is there's this gang of professional robbers, and because they're robbers they go around robbing different places, and because of that they get chased by the police, and they escape, and then they get chased again, and I don't think there's any need to make all this effort to watch because it's the same old story as in those movies they sometimes show on the TV in the evenings. I can't help wondering what's so interesting, and I keep sneaking a glance at Tutti next to me, and she's completely focused on the movie and doesn't notice I'm looking at her. Every time there's some movement on the screen, a tiny bit of light flickers in the wet part of Tutti's eyes.

In the film the men talk and get angry, and then there's this other man, and a woman comes and they have an argument and swear at each other, and there's this girl about our age or a little bit older who cries, and there are loads of cars, and they drive, and they get angry, and they escape and they run, and then there's a chase again, and it goes on like this over and over again. I'm trying to watch as carefully as I can, but from time to time a yawn escapes and I strain my eyes trying to read the display on the DVD player to see how much time is left, but I can never quite make out the little numbers.

Just around maybe the middle of the film, the gang of robbers decides to do one last job, but it doesn't go well, and they get into a really wild gunfight with the police. The instant they start shooting, Tutti's whole body is suddenly bubbling with energy—I can almost feel it just from sitting next to her—and she leans forward in her seat, and I watch her reflected in the light, hardly blinking, as if she doesn't want to miss even a split second of what is happening, her eyes gleaming as she takes it all in.

The scene is really loud, the men keep firing like crazy at both friends and enemies, it doesn't seem to matter. Glass smashing, bullets hitting cars, and on top of that people screaming. In the middle of all this, the robbers are hauling bags of stolen banknotes on their shoulders, trying to get to the getaway car, and they're desperate and firing their guns over and over, but as there are far more police than robbers, and more policemen appearing all the time, one of the robbers gets shot and falls to the ground, and someone else is injured and tries to crawl away but then stops moving, and only two members of the gang manage to escape. It must hurt getting shot by one of those long black guns, I think. Blood comes spurting out, and I wonder how that feels. I wonder how heavy the bags were stuffed with all that money. When they use the money will somebody know that it was stolen? I'm thinking about all these things as I try to keep watching all the action and confusion on the screen. Finally the gunfight ends and the car drives away, and then all of a sudden it's a completely different scene and Tutti lets out a big sigh, grabs the remote, and pauses the DVD.

"Isn't that cool?"

Tutti's face is shiny with the light from the TV screen, one half of it is sort of blue, and she looks kind of different from the usual Tutti. Her nostrils are a little wider, and she is very excited.

"I really love that scene!" she says confidently and looks right into my face. "What did you think?"

"Well," I say, shifting my bum a bit on the sofa. "It was a bit, kind of, violent."

Tutti looks at me like she's saying *what the hell was that?* and sighs. Then she makes her eyes all narrow and glares at me.

"Well, obviously it's violent," she says, turning right round to face me and speaking super slowly and carefully as if she's making sure I understand every word. "Anyone can see that. I mean the sounds. It's the sounds that are really awesome, and also what they do with their bodies when they shoot the guns."

"The sound was definitely awesome," I say.

"And the shape of their bodies?"

"The shape of their bodies was awesome too."

"Right?"

In my mind I'm hoping she isn't about to ask me exactly what part was awesome, and my heart's thumping, but it looks like she's satisfied with my answers, and she laughs happily.

"I've been watching that gunfight scene at least twice a week for years now."

"Honest?"

"Honest to God. Anyway I just love that gun battle so much, I can't stop watching it."

"Is it because you want to do it that you like it so much?" I ask, without really thinking.

"What do you mean?"

"I mean I thought it might be because you want to try running around shooting a gun like that."

Tutti stared at me, her mouth open in shock. "No! No way! How could you even think something like that? The point is, even I don't know why I love that scene so much."

I nod without saying anything.

"I've seen tons of movies with gunfights, and they're all amazing, but I haven't seen any with such awesome sound. And I like that they really give it all they got."

"Yeah, they really give it all they got," I say, nodding gravely.

"Anyway, I like it so much I can do this," says Tutti, standing up and moving several piles of magazines from around the sofa to the side of the room, clearing the widest path between the sofa and the TV.

"Are you ready? Watch."

She picks up the remote and presses the REWIND button until she's got the disc to the right place, then presses the PLAY button and tosses the remote onto the sofa. *Here we go*, she says, and the very next moment that the gunfight scene starts, Tutti is in front of the screen—I'm not sure how to explain this—but she's begun to act out the actions of the people in the film, and every single one of her movements is exactly, absolutely perfectly, the same as on the screen behind her, and her timing is *amazing*.

I'm totally stunned and I sit there watching Tutti with my mouth hanging open. She syncs her movements with the sound of the gunshots on the TV, and posing her body in the same way as each of the robbers and the policemen as the screen changes, she keeps on shooting. She stretches out her arm and blasts her gun over and over, then in the next instant crouches down to avoid the fire, throws herself into a body roll, then just like the people in the movie she does this *clatter clatter clatter* thing with her gun, then brings it back up high, braces her legs, and starts firing even more furiously. Tutti's eyes as she glares at her enemy are incredible. Of course, you can't see a gun, but there is the sound of Tutti firing, her performing each person's movements with absolute precision, and she's playing several different roles, going from one to the next without stopping. She never gets lost, she's acting every sound, every person, everything is there in her movements. It's perfect, maybe too perfect. In fact, seeing how perfect she is, I begin to feel a little bit scared and I want to shout *enough!* or *stop!*, and the words have climbed up into my throat but I swallow them back down, and I don't know why, but I can't take my eyes off Tutti. The gunfight scene is long. It's so long that for some reason I find myself wanting to cry, and I suddenly remember Tutti's dad, and I look over and I see he's got his head tipped back, his mouth open, and his neck is on the back of the sofa and he's fast asleep. He looks exactly as if he's just been shot by Tutti, and this thought makes me feel even more like crying, and the gun battle is getting even faster and furiouser, and as I watch Tutti, as she continues to fit her movements perfectly to the sound and the action, I realize that I'm kneeling on the sofa with both of my hands over my chest, my fingers tightly locked together.

"That was awesome!" I say, and I really mean it.

"Yeah, not bad," replies Tutti, with a so-so kind of expression, but then she looks at me and grins.

Tutti offers to walk with me as far as where the pop vending machine is, so the two of us set out side by side along the street, which looks like a completely different place at night without anybody around. It's right before the end of summer and you can see tiny black insects buzzing around the hazy white light of the street lights. Tutti has made me perform the gunfight scene with her, and I was really nervous but I gave it a try and I don't know how it happened but I got so into it that it ended up being around ten thirty by the time I left her house. Tutti's dad slept all through our scene, he woke up in time to see us off at the door, but then he went straight back to the living room.

"You might have some talent there, I'm not sure yet, but anyway, why don't you come and practise the gunfight with me again?"

"OK!"

It's right then I suddenly remember that Tutti doesn't have a mother. I think of the house I was just in with its messy living room, and Tutti's dad asleep on the sofa with his mouth open. I've never heard anything directly from Tutti about her mum, we've never talked about it, but somehow everyone in the class knows that her mother died of an illness when Tutti was very young. I'm pretty sure that everyone in the class must know about my dad too, but not one person has ever asked me about him, so I've never talked about him to anyone. As I'm walking with Tutti I start to feel like talking about all that, I don't know why. There doesn't feel like there's all that much to say, and yet I still want to say something about it. But what does talking about it mean exactly, and what should I start by asking, and would the conversation go something like *you don't have a mum, right?* and then that would be the end, so really it'd make no difference whether we talked about it or not, and this is what I'm thinking, and in the end I realize we've arrived at the vending machine without me ever managing to say anything.

"Thanks for inviting me to watch the movie," I say. "It was fun."

"I had fun too."

"Yeah," I say.

"You know that was the first time I ever showed me doing that to anyone besides my dad."

"Really? You know if you did that at school, everyone would think you were totally cool."

"But everyone's so good at dance and stuff. And I think probably anybody could do it."

"No way!" I say, very seriously. "If you're talking about dance, you mean what those three girls do? What you just showed me, they can't even compare to you. What you did is so totally way, way more awesome than anything they do."

Tutti looks a little embarrassed. Then, moving her mouth in a strange way, maybe on purpose, she says, *Really? Do you really think so?* in a tiny voice, and I say, *Yes, I do, really.*

"Well, then you'd better come back again and watch. He's the best—Al Pacino!" she says, a big grin on her face.

"What's that?"

"You know—the film we just saw—Lieutenant Hanna. Al Pacino plays him."

"Oh, it's somebody's name. I thought it might be how you say goodbye in some other country."

"That'd be cool too."

As I start home she waves at me and says, *Al Pacino!* I raise my hand and wave back and say, *Al Pacino!* And then all of a sudden it seems very funny and we both burst out laughing at the exact same time, and we get louder and louder until we're both bent double laughing our heads off. And as we're laughing, lights appear out of nowhere and get bigger and closer, and a car roars past us.

"OK, I'm going home," says Tutti, panting, catching her breath, and right at that moment I decide I'm going to talk to her about it, well, I don't exactly *decide*, because there isn't even a second to think about it, but in that moment all that comes out of my mouth are two words.

"About sandwiches..."

"Sandwiches?"

"No, not sandwiches exactly, I mean, that shop inside the supermarket where they sell sandwiches, that corner where they sell them..."

I swallow hard and try to keep going, but I don't really know how to explain, so I just go silent. Tutti looks straight at me and says, *Yes, I know it*, then she stands there waiting for me to find the next words.

"There's this woman who works at that sandwich counter."

"Yes, there is."

"There is, right?"

"There is."

"There is. And I call that woman Ms Ice Sandwich."

"OK," says Tutti, nodding.

"I heard a rumour the other day at school, you know, about Ms Ice Sandwich."

Tutti thinks for a moment. "About her face?"

"Yes," I say. I've been staring at the ground the whole time, but now I look up at Tutti. "Well... So... someone was talking about her face, and I'm not sure what it means."

"What it means?"

"Yeah, like what they meant."

"Perhaps I should ask, what is it between you and Ms Ice Sandwich? I mean, do you like have some kind of a *relationship*?"

Being asked about a *relationship* makes me silent again. I don't have any kind of a *relationship* with her, have never said anything to her except order a sandwich—and here I am wondering why I'm even having this conversation with Tutti, I don't have any idea. Just as I'm thinking this, and feeling like there's nothing more I can do to explain, out comes from me this strange sigh that I don't understand. Then I say, *It's not exactly a relationship, but...* and then I break off... and then I try to explain about how I went to see Ms Ice Sandwich through the summer, and about how she does her job, and all about those cool eyes, and everything.

Tutti's voice turns strangely quiet.

"So you really like Ms Ice Sandwich, then?"

I play her words over in my head, in the same strange, quiet little voice. And I nod.

"Oh."

I can't think of any way to respond to her *oh*, and Tutti doesn't say anything more either. We stand there in silence until we see someone walking towards us from the direction of Tutti's house, and it's Tutti's dad. *My dad's coming to get me*, Tutti says, *I'd better go*, and she smiles and waves goodbye. She starts to walk towards her father and then suddenly turns back as if she's remembered something. *Al Pacino!* she calls out and waves again.

When I get home my mum comes out of the salon saying, *It's late, you had me worried.* I thought she might be angry with me because of the time, but she doesn't seem to be bothered at all and instead just says, *Are you going to take a bath?* I tell her not tonight and I go to Grandma's room. I hear the salon door shut. Grandma's asleep. I look at the time and I see it's almost eleven o'clock, but I'm not even a little bit tired yet. I stand by Grandma's bed and look at her face as she's sleeping, then I pull up a *zabuton* cushion and sit on the floor, scratching the skin around the scabs on my knees until it turns red, then I stand up again and look at Grandma's sleeping face. I check the clock again, but barely any time has passed at all.

In Grandma's room, which seems to be floating somewhere in the noiseless night, in this room with just Grandma and me in it, I get out my sketchbook and open it up on the *kotatsu* table, and I pick up my pencil and start moving it across the blank paper. I draw a bunch of faint pencil lines round and round in a circle, and the lines become stronger and stronger until they finally become Ms Ice Sandwich's face. Her big eyes. Her tight-fitting hair. The place where the front fringe bit and the side bits meet. But I notice that up until now I've had no trouble seeing her face in my mind, I've always been able to remember all the important parts, but now there are bits and pieces of her face that I've forgotten. I draw a little more, then a little bit more, but when I look at the whole thing, there's something wrong with it—it doesn't look like Ms Ice Sandwich. In other words, the Ms Ice Sandwich I'm drawing doesn't look like the real Ms Ice Sandwich, but I can't tell why that is.

I stare at the white part of the sliding-screen doors, and try to make the face of Ms Ice Sandwich, who I haven't seen in a long time, come back to me. And I realize that I really have to concentrate now to make it come back. I flip over the page of my sketchbook, turn to a new page, and start drawing Ms Ice Sandwich's face again from the beginning. This time I start with her head. Then I add the outline of her face, then...

As I move my pencil, I remember the way she grabs the sandwiches with her silver pincers and slips them into the plastic bags. How cool she is. How skilful and strong she is. How she stood there and glared at that man who was yelling at her. Her long arms. Her sharp expression. And her big eyes. The dogs. The dogs who run along the road made of bricks. The dogs with the giant eyes who run around a castle somewhere. The princess—that's right! Those dogs with the great big eyes like Ms Ice Sandwich are running with a princess on their back. They are running off to some place, carrying a beautiful princess with a long dress, the skirt flying in the wind. Ms Ice Sandwich is running off to some place. Her big eyes wider than ever, on her back the princess in the long dress, it's Ms Ice Sandwich who's running.

I keep drawing Ms Ice Sandwich deep into the night. This is the most time I've ever spent, and it's the most complicated, but of all the pictures I've ever drawn of her, this is the one that looks the most like the Ms Ice Sandwich that I know, or anyway that's how it feels. After I'm done drawing, I take a blue crayon and carefully colour in her eyelids. I take the drawing, which isn't finished yet, and slide it gently between two pages of my sketchbook, then I look down at my hands and see that they're smudged with pencil and crayon. I try to rub them off, and start thinking about what happened today. It feels like a lot happened, but also that a lot didn't happen. Tutti's gunfight. Her being totally cool. The Christmas tree with the tilted star. The smell of curry. The piles of magazines. And then Tutti asking me if I liked Ms Ice Sandwich. The noise of the car driving past. Tutti's dad coming out of the shadows to get her. And now I'm beginning to feel so drained and tired that I don't think I can move. I don't even wash my hands and face, I just curl up on the floor and close my eyes, and my eyelids start to get heavy and I can't open my eyes any more. I wonder if when I wake up will I be on my futon, and how nice it will be if I am. I remember a long time ago, maybe before I could have any memories, so it could be a memory that I made up, someone like my dad, when I was half-asleep, picking me up and rocking me and laying me down on my soft futon, and it feels like a real memory that comes back to me at times like this, and maybe tomorrow morning I will find myself tucked up in my futon. I know it's not going to happen, still I think about it because it feels like I am remembering my dad. I hear myself mumbling, *Did you bring me here when I was sleepy?* I realize that I am speaking to my dad who isn't here, but he must be here somewhere. And I remember the sensation of being in his arms as I fall asleep with my head on the *zabuton*.

AT **SCHOOL,** whether our eyes meet or not, Tutti acts kind of cold and doesn't seem to want to talk to me. It's not that she's being mean or anything, just cold, or like she's avoiding me, not enough for me to ask her what's up or anything, but there's a new feeling of distance between us. But when I think about it, it's not like up till now at school Tutti and I have always been pals, or chatted to each other, so maybe I'm misinterpreting her behaviour and I'm just overreacting. But even if this is the right explanation, I have no idea what to do about it, and every day ends up being one awkward day after the one before.

I don't go to see Ms Ice Sandwich either. Even when I pass close by the supermarket on my way home from school, I never get the urge to go inside. Instead, I work a little every day on my Ms Ice Sandwich portrait. I experiment with coloured pencils and crayons and felt-tip pens to get the colour right, starting over many times, and gradually day by day, I remember her face and transfer the image I see inside my head onto paper. Mum's the same as ever, in the salon with her ladies, talking and crying, and she's always playing with her mobile phone or her computer. I keep on spending time sitting in Grandma's room drawing my picture.

Things go on like this for about a month. One day I'm on my way home from school with Doo-Wop, and I've just said, *See you tomorrow*, and we're going our separate ways when Tutti suddenly steps out from behind a telegraph pole, surprising me.

"Long time no see!" says Tutti.

"Yeah," I say, "long time."

The truth is it hasn't been long at all, since we see each other every day at school, so it's a sort of weird greeting that we say anyway.

"It really feels like it," she says.

"Yeah, it really feels like it," I say.

We start strolling in the direction of our houses, chatting about tests, and our teacher's strange habits, and the fable that we studied in Japanese class. We get to the bench and for once nobody's sitting there, and without saying anything we both sit down. Tutti hangs her backpack over one end of the bench, takes off her shoes and holds them upside down and shakes the grit out of them. A whole load of grit, way more than I expected, comes pouring out, and it makes me laugh. She tells me about her visit to the planetarium on Sunday, and I tell her about the video game that Doo-Wop is still obsessed with, and we talk about how boring morning assembly is. Then, after we've talked about all these different things, Tutti makes a sighing sound, and gets a determined expression on her face.

"Ms Ice Sandwich," she says.

I'm startled by these words out of Tutti's mouth. I turn to look at her.

She looks me straight in the eyes and says it again: "Ms Ice Sandwich."

"Ms Ice Sandwich," I repeat, exactly the way she's just said it.

"Ms Ice Sandwich, what's happened about her?" she asks, very serious.

"What's happened...? Nothing's happened. Nothing at all's happened."

"So you haven't gone to see her?"

"No, not once."

"Why not?"

"I don't know, I just haven't."

"The other day you asked me about the rumours and stuff about her face."

"Yeah."

"That's where the conversation ended, but you gave me the feeling you wanted to say something else," says Tutti, looking right at me.

"That was..." I start to say, but I get stuck.

Tutti patiently doesn't say anything.

"That was... well... about her face, I mean, those girls in the class were saying if they had a face like that they wanted to die, or they couldn't live any more, you know, that sort of thing, and I was shocked, and I was thinking what did they mean by that, you know, I was thinking about that..."

"And it made you angry?"

"No, I don't think that was it," I say. "I think that when I heard them saying things like that about her face that I'd been looking at for a long time, I was surprised."

"Just surprised?"

I sit and think some more about this. Yeah, I was surprised but I also felt sad and maybe frightened, and on top of that, I was... I was worried about Ms Ice Sandwich, like was she all right, and I start to say to Tutti, "When I thought about them talking about Ms Ice Sandwich that way..." and I still can't finish the sentence.

"OK then," says Tutti, who unexpectedly slaps me on the shoulder. "Do you never want to see Ms Ice Sandwich again? Is that what you want?"

"What are you talking about?" I ask, stunned.

"What I said."

"You mean, never see her again forever?"

"Exactly."

"Why?"

"Why?" Tutti looks amazed that I don't know why. "You haven't gone to see her, not for ages. And if it goes on like that forever, then you'll never see her again."

I'm speechless.

"I'm right, right?" Tutti stares at me like she thinks I'm dumb. "Because that's what's going to happen. When you say *see you tomorrow* to someone, it's because you're going to keep seeing them. It's like at school you see everybody because they go to school every day. But when you graduate and you don't go to school any more, it stops and you don't see everybody any more. If you want to see somebody, you have to make plans to meet, or even make plans to make plans, and next thing you end up not seeing them any more. That's what's going to happen. If you don't see somebody, you end up never seeing them. And then there's going to be nothing left of them at all."

I'm listening, still not saying a word.

"The worst thing is, you never know when somebody's going to just disappear."

"Huh?"

"Yes, disappear, like go away and never come back. You never see them again. You want to see them but it's too late, they're gone."

Tutti pauses, kind of smiles.

"And the ones who disappear, they don't know that they're going to. They disappear without knowing. Just like that. They go away and then nobody sees them any more."

I sit there, maybe nodding.

"I stopped doing that kind of thing a long time ago," Tutti says. "You know—putting off stuff and not doing anything, and not going and seeing somebody when I really wanted to. I stopped that. It's too risky... You should just go and see someone when you can, right?"

"When did you figure that out?"

"When I was in first grade. And I wrote it down."

"Really? You're smart."

"Nah, not that smart. But there's loads of hard stuff in life, and maybe when we're grown-ups, there's going to be tons more hard stuff to deal with. And when that happens, I'm going to tell myself I can't give in or freeze up and get discouraged and do nothing. I have to believe that. Because I've already had to deal with the hardest thing in the world. You know what that was?"

"What?"

"It was to try to meet someone who's already disappeared."

"Oh," I say. "Yeah."

"Right?"

Tutti looks at me and forces a kind of laugh. We sit for a while without speaking. A woman I've seen around comes by, walking her Yorkshire terrier, pausing to say hello as the dog sniffs around Tutti's feet and Tutti pets its small brown head. The woman tugs on the dog's leash, and Tutti says, *See you later*.

"So," Tutti says, turning back to me, "you really have to go and see Ms Ice Sandwich."

I don't say anything.

"You have to."

I still don't say anything.

"You understand why, don't you?"

"I do. I do, but..."

"But what?"

"No, it's nothing," I say, inhaling through my nose and staring down at the toes of my trainers.

"And you have to go and not just look at her, you have to *see* her, and that means you have to *meet* her."

"I'm not just going to buy a sandwich from her?"

"That's what I've been trying to tell you. You have to *meet* her," Tutti says firmly.

"How am I going to meet her?" I ask, already feeling butterflies in my stomach.

"You can start with *nice to meet you*."

Then Tutti and I discussed how to do this (to be honest, it was mostly me listening to her) and the plan was to go to the supermarket the next day. I said that it was too soon but she ignored me, and before I knew it we had a time set up.

The next day I walk into the supermarket just behind Tutti, feeling really nervous. I haven't been here in over a month, but it feels as if I've entered a time warp, and it's just like the summer holidays again when I used to come here every day.

I peek at the sandwich counter from the eggs, but I can't see Ms Ice Sandwich. *She's not here*, I whisper to Tutti, and she whispers back, *Has this ever happened before?* Me: *No, never.* Tutti: *Maybe she took the day off.* And so that day we give up and go home. The following day is exactly the same—we go to the supermarket and watch from behind the eggs, but there's no sign of Ms Ice Sandwich.

We go across the road to the chemist's and I sit down on the steps by the entrance.

"You were right—she disappeared," I tell Tutti, feeling very let down.

Tutti stands there, like she's thinking. I don't have any strength left in my body, my head feels all fuzzy like when I catch a cold, and my feet feel weird, kind of wobbly on the ground. Then, without saying a single word, Tutti turns and walks back towards the supermarket. I think she must be going to get pop from the vending machine, but she doesn't stop there and goes right through the front door. I sit and watch the door and see mostly people I don't know go in and come out, and then every so often a face I recognize. But none of them notices me, and for some reason I feel a little bit relieved.

Tutti's been gone a while, and I'm staring at the ground when a pair of trainers come into view. I look up to see Tutti.

"I did it," she says.

"Did what?"

"I went in and asked. About Ms Ice Sandwich. Why she wasn't there."

I jump up from the step. "Wh— who did you ask?"

"One of the people who works there," she replies. Then after a pause, she says, "Ms Ice Sandwich doesn't work there any more."

I can't believe what I'm hearing, and I stare at Tutti.

"But they told me she's coming back to pick up her stuff," she explains.

"Did they tell you when?"

"Monday, they said. Next Monday."

"Next Monday," I say, as if it's a new word.

"Right. Next Monday," she repeats after me. "I told them I had something for her, and they told me she was going to be here next Monday evening."

"Next Monday."

"Next Monday evening."

Tutti and I start walking back under a heavy cloud of feeling, silently. At the point where we have to go separate ways, Tutti suddenly says, *It's good you found out today.* Then in a much quieter voice, *You're going on Monday, right?* I don't have an answer so I say nothing. Tutti looks at me, waiting, then she gives up. She sighs, presses one hand to her forehead, then raises her other hand in goodbye, and without a word turns towards her house. She walks so her backpack bounces, and her heels scrape the ground as she gets farther along her way. I call out, *Tutti!* She slowly turns around, and I wave and shout, *Al Pacino!* Tutti is gripping the waist belt of her backpack, and she doesn't respond or do anything, then she turns and starts walking again. I shout, *Al Pacino!* once more. She turns around again, starts walking backwards, very slowly, her eyes on me. After a few moments, in a kind of small voice, she calls out *Al Pacino*, and disappears around the corner.

I 'LL SEE MS ICE SANDWICH on the day after the day after tomorrow, and that'll probably be the last time I ever see her. I think about this as I do my homework, watch some kind of boring TV, eat dinner, talk to Mum a bit, and then go into Grandma's room to work some more on my picture. I keep thinking, *Monday will be the last time I ever see her*, but I can't come to grips with what *Monday will be the last time I ever see her* means.

I stop thinking about it and concentrate on drawing Ms Ice Sandwich's picture. At one point, I thought I was finished with it, but I see now there are still lots of things left to do. I take my pencil and draw in every hair on her head, and with a fine-point pen I draw her eyelashes in one by one, rub them out with my fingers, then draw them again, then I take bright electric-blue watercolour and paint over the blue crayon on her eyelids, kind of filling in the gaps. The blue crayon repels the paint, but I keep on patiently painting.

Finally, by Sunday night, Ms Ice Sandwich's picture feels done. I go over and stand by Grandma's bed, holding the painting in front of my chest.

"Grandma, this is my portrait of Ms Ice Sandwich. This is the best picture I've ever drawn. Don't you think? It looks just like Ms Ice Sandwich. The Ms Ice Sandwich I'm always talking to you about. See those cool eyes? I made them really beautiful, it looks just like her. And guess what? After tomorrow, Ms Ice Sandwich isn't going to be there any more. It's her last day. Tutti asked someone at the supermarket for me."

As I ramble on like this to Grandma, I start to feel a pain in my chest and tears suddenly start to roll down my cheeks, and suddenly I'm crying my eyes out. I'm not sure what's causing it, why I'm so unhappy, but I can't stop the tears. The angel decorations in Mum's salon, or the smell of the blue crayon, the pattern on the *zabuton* cover that I trace with the tip of my finger, Tutti's backpack getting farther into the distance, maybe all of this—everything inside me feels scrambled. Every time I breathe, my body kind of shudders and I feel like I'm never going to stop crying. With one hand on the sheet of Grandma's bed, I squat down with my knees pulled up to my chin, and my other hand covering my eyes, and I stay like that crying and crying. I cry so hard that my shoulders heave and my face is soaked in tears and snot. And then I feel something touch my head, which startles me. I stop and look up and see that it's Grandma. Grandma who's supposed to be asleep is awake and her little eyes are looking at me tenderly and she's got a faint smile on her face and her hand is gently resting on my head. She looks kindly into my face and there's a little trembling glow in the pupils of her eyes, then in a really, really tiny voice, she says, *Don't cry*. Very quietly, I say, *Grandma*, and I reach up to touch her but I don't stop crying. We stay that way for a while before I end up falling asleep on the *zabuton*.

After school the next day, I collect my painting of Ms Ice Sandwich from home, and go to the supermarket. There's no sign of Ms Ice Sandwich at the sandwich counter. Tutti had said *Monday evening*. I don't know what time in the evening exactly, but I guess that if I wait here, if she is coming, I'll see her. The supermarket starts getting crowded, so I go outside and stand in a spot where I can watch the front entrance as well as the big doors on the side where the trolleys and the deliveries go in and out, and I wait, watching for Ms Ice Sandwich to appear.

After waiting I don't know how long, the side doors open and *it's Ms Ice Sandwich!* But for some reason my feet won't move, and I stand there watching that face, that head of dark hair move steadily away from me. She stops to say something to some people carrying cardboard boxes, speaks to someone else walking by, then she waves and sets off down the street towards the station. My feet suddenly able to move, I take off after her. I catch up with her halfway between the supermarket and the station and walk up so I'm next to her and I say, *Um, excuse me, Miss?*

Surprised, Ms Ice Sandwich turns to look at me. *Me?* she asks. *Yes,* I answer. I bow a little. *What is it?* she asks, stepping to the very edge of the road so she isn't in the way of all the people walking by. Her eyes are so big, and her eyelids are coloured her usual electric ice-blue. My own eyes are wide open as I stare at her face. I begin by saying, *I used to come to your shop to buy sandwiches.* Ms Ice Sandwich: *Oh yes, I thought I'd seen you before.* Me: *I heard you're leaving that shop.* Ms Ice

Sandwich: *That's right*. Me: *Really?* Ms Ice Sandwich: *Yes, I am*. At that point I don't know what to say, so I just hand her my picture, rolled up and fastened with a rubber band. *This... this is a picture I drew*, I say. Ms Ice Sandwich: *Really? May I look at it?*, and she removes the rubber band and unrolls the picture. *Wow!* Ms Ice Sandwich says, sounding genuinely surprised. *Is this me?* Me: *Yes, it is*. Ms Ice Sandwich: *It's really me?* Me: *Yes!* Ms Ice Sandwich: *You drew it for me?* Me: *Yes, I did!* I'm trying frantically to respond properly, but I feel my face burning hotter and hotter, and I can't even believe I'm standing here talking to Ms Ice Sandwich, yet here I am talking to her, and every time I think about it my face gets even hotter.

"Can I keep this?" asks Ms Ice Sandwich.

"Yes."

"Thank you. You know," she goes on, "I think you're going to be an artist in the future." She laughs happily.

This is the first time I have ever seen Ms Ice Sandwich laugh like that.

"And I remember now, you always came to buy sandwiches from me, so thank you for that too."

"It was nothing," I say, shaking my head.

"This is a nice town. I worked here quite a long time. I really liked it."

"Are y— are you really leaving?"

"Yes. I'm getting married and going to live somewhere else."

"You're getting married?"

"That's right."

"Oh," I say, nodding my head like mad.

"Well, I'd better get going," says Ms Ice Sandwich. "Thank you for the picture. Take care of yourself!"

There's a black part of the asphalt, and there's a dark grey part, and they run into one another, and they feel hard under the soles of my shoes as ever.

The supermarket car park, jam-packed with cars. The rounded, coloured neon letters on the dry cleaner's signboard. The face of a politician that completely fills a rectangular poster. The broken white line along the edge of the road, its paint worn off in places. The leaflets and advertisements overflowing the postbox of the old house where nobody lives any more. The weeds I don't know the name of. The man who sells vegetables stuffed in cardboard boxes from his truck. The bench where me and Tutti saw the Yorkshire terrier. The big barrel in someone's garden that's full of water (I have no idea what it's for). The notices pinned to the community bulletin board. The tip of the faded surfboard sticking out from the balcony of a second-floor apartment. A potted plant. A tricycle in front of a door. A nameplate. A manhole. Gates and rubbish bins. I notice all these different things on the route back.

When I get home, Mum is giving Grandma her dinner. *Hi, let's have dinner together,* she says, and I say, *Yes.* Mum says, *You look really tired, are you OK? I hope you haven't caught a cold. You know, it's fine to draw pictures and be in Grandma's room, but you need to sleep properly on your own futon.* I say *yes* again, and I sit at the table and eat my dinner, and I take a bath as Mum tells me, get into my pyjamas, and go into the bedroom.

You really don't look well, says Mum as she does her stretches, and I answer something vague. Then I mumble, *I'm going to sleep,* and turn down the cover of my futon and climb in. That's when Mum says, *Before you go to sleep, here, I've got this for you,* and she brings over a largish, square package and hands it to me.

"What is it?" I ask, sitting up.

"Open it and see."

I tear off the thin brown-paper packaging. "It's a book!"

"You know how you were asking me about it? The picture book about the dogs with the giant eyes? I couldn't find a book with just that story, but this collection has the story in it. Look, isn't it this one?"

Mum flips through the pages and shows me a picture of the dogs.

"Yes," I say. "This is the one! Mum, this is it!"

That night, tucked in my futon, in the dim light of the bedroom, I read *The Tinderbox* over and over. Just as I remembered, in the pictures the dogs with enormous eyes run with a princess on their backs. As I look at the pictures, they're very familiar, like a fond memory of my own. I'm not sure whether I really came across this story or these illustrations before, but I have to believe that back when I was a little boy, someone read this book to me. I mean, that must be how I already know the story, and how I know these dogs with big eyes. I'm still looking at the pictures when I fall asleep.

That night, I dream. A dream where the dogs with the giant eyes carry the princess on their back and they're running around the town. I'm watching them from somewhere high up and far away. Under a spreading, starry sky, they take off from the brick road and they fly, their eyes growing bigger and bigger. Their breathing is rough, they're panting, and they come right up to me with those gleaming rows of fangs as big as gates. Next I'm running with the dogs, at the same speed, all over the town. And now I realize I've turned into one of the three dogs, and my huge paws covered in brown fur are growing by the second, and my paws make a loud kind of *clack* as they kick off from the bricks, and they send off sparks, and I'm using every ounce of strength in my body to run towards the castle. The skirt of the princess's long dress brushes against my back. I turn around as I'm running to check that the princess is all right. Lying on my back, wearing a long white dress, it's Ms Ice Sandwich. She has a spellbound expression on her face, her eyes with their electric ice-blue lids are shut tight, and she's lying on my back. She strokes the fur on my neck with her long, fair right hand, with her left she has a firm grip on my shoulder blade. Ms Ice Sandwich is on my back and we sparkle as we dash through the town, heading towards the castle. I'm watching this whole scene, my eyes wide in wonder. Ms Ice Sandwich on my back, flying into the wind, striding through the night, past gawping crowds of people, shaking off expectations, with little bursts of laughter, heading towards the castle. A soft smile on her lips, Ms Ice Sandwich lies secure and safe on my back. My eyes grow even more gigantic, taking in everything around me as we run through the night. I exhale a white cloud of breath from between my fangs, and the clear liquid that drips from my nose makes Ms Ice Sandwich's dress wet, creating a spot that then quickly vanishes. Baring my fangs, I kick off from the rooftops, breathing out into the night, faster than anybody, stronger than anybody, Ms Ice Sandwich on my back, I run through the night. My claws spray gazillions of sparks as I run towards the castle. *Goodbye, Ms Ice Sandwich! Goodbye, Ms Ice Sandwich!* The hem of her dress falls over my eyes, then blows away again, finally the town stops rushing by so quickly, and my body begins to slow down second by second. My legs become heavier and heavier, and with a great rumbling of the earth, my body is released into a big open space, and now I can't move on the bricks any more, and I just stand there breathing in and out. And as I watch my belly heaving, my eyelids become weighted down, and before long my giant eyes have stopped watching everything. *Goodbye.* There's the sound of someone breathing, that's what I'm listening to. *Goodbye.* The stars are setting, and in their last breath somebody tells me *goodbye.* Someone is saying *goodbye*, and now I can't move at all, and all

I can do is hold my breath, and silently listen to the final sound, nothing to do but listen silently to the very last echo of that sound.

I TOLD EVERYONE in my class that they didn't need to come to my grandma's funeral, but Tutti shows up, along with her dad. It's a beautiful, sunny day towards the end of December, and your breath comes out so white it looks like you can touch it. By the time I run into Tutti, I've already stopped crying, and I lift my hand a little, and at first she looks a bit uncomfortable but then she lifts her hand a bit too. *Thanks for coming,* I say to her, and she says, *No problem,* shaking her head. After the funeral service, everyone eats a bento together, then we have to do some greetings, and then some of the relatives and Mum and me get into the hearse and go to the crematorium. Grandma looks very small and white when she's brought back out. She's only bones and ash, which are gathered up and put into a pretty box. I hug her tightly to my chest.

In the new year, Tutti and I start going to the planetarium, or to have ice cream, or I go to her house to watch movies. My voice sometimes gets a bit scratchy, and Tutti starts growing very quickly, and soon she's way taller than me. The gunfight that we perform in Tutti's living room gets even more polished, and her dad is always there napping on the sofa. Doo-Wop is still crazy about the same old video game, and my mum seems to be crazy about the same old stuff too, sitting in her salon listening to all these different women talking, crying, and laughing.

Sometimes I go to the supermarket just to buy sandwiches from the sandwich shop. There's always the same woman behind the glass case, and when I say, *May I have one egg sandwich, please,* she smiles at me, puts it into a plastic bag, and places it firmly in my hand. I say, *Thank you,* and then, *I think I'll have another one, please,* and I give her some more money. We haven't made any plans today, but I think I'll go over to Tutti's house. And if Tutti's there, we can sit on the sofa together and eat egg sandwiches.

JAPANESE FICTION
AVAILABLE AND COMING SOON
FROM PUSHKIN PRESS

MS ICE SANDWICH
Mieko Kawakami

MURDER IN THE AGE OF ENLIGHTENMENT
Ryūnosuke Akutagawa

THE HONJIN MURDERS
Seishi Yokomizo

RECORD OF A NIGHT TOO BRIEF
Hiromi Kawakami

SPRING GARDEN
Tomoka Shibasaki

COIN LOCKER BABIES
Ryu Murakami

THE DECAGON HOUSE MURDERS
Yukito Ayatsuji

SLOW BOAT
Hideo Furukawa

THE HUNTING GUN
Yasushi Inoue

SALAD ANNIVERSARY
Machi Tawara

THE CAKE TREE IN THE RUINS
Akiyuki Nosaka